When the grass in the hay field was ready, the farmer hooked the
mower to the tractor and cut swath after swath around the field.

After drying, the grass was rolled into windrows with a hay rake.

HAYSTACK

BONNIE and ARTHUR GEISERT

HOUGHTON MIFFLIN COMPANY BOSTON

1995

For our parents

Walter Lorraine (wl) Books

Geisert, Bonnie.
    Haystack / by Bonnie Geisert and Arthur Geisert.
        p.   cm.
    ISBN 0-395-69722-0
    1. Hay—Juvenile literature.   2. Stacks (Hay, grain, etc.)—
Juvenile literature.   3. Hay as feed—Juvenile literature.
[1. Hay.   2. Farm life.]   I. Geisert, Arthur.   II. Title.
SB198.G45   1995
633.2'086—dc20   94-7684
                                CIP
                                AC

Printed in the United States of America
HOR   10   9   8   7   6   5   4   3   2   1

H A Y S T A C K

In a time not so long ago, before machines made hay in
convenient bundles, haystacks stood high, long, and wide
on the prairie.

Across the prairie in the spring, the grass grew tall.

The hydraulic lift with its hay basket was attached to the tractor
and the windrows were bunched into piles.

Pile after pile was brought to the center of the field, where a frame
was built for the haystack.

The haystack grew quickly.

Everyone in the family helped. The hay was spread evenly with pitchforks.

As the haystack grew higher, tromping packed the hay
so that the whole field would fit.

There was time to rest while waiting for the loads of hay.

When the last hay from the field was collected, the haystack was done.

It was a very large stack of hay.

It would feed the cattle for the rest of the year.

Thunderstorms threatened the haystack.

ning, the haystack could catch fire and burn to the ground.

On hot days, the haystack shaded the cattle from the sun.

If hit by lightning, the haystack could catch fire and burn to the ground.

On hot days, the haystack shaded the cattle from the sun.

The cattle ate as far as they could reach. Then, the hay was pitched down to them.

Before winter, the frame was removed.

Now the cattle could reach the hay.

They stayed close to the haystack through the winter.

They were protected from the cold winter wind and they had food whenever
they wanted.

Near the end of winter, when it was time for the calves to be born,
the cattle were herded to another field.

The pigs and their piglets were moved to the hay field.

Now they had the field to run in.

And they had the food from the haystack.

The haystack was a place to feed and a place to rest.

After some weeks, the cattle and new calves were herded back into the hay field. They shared the last of the hay with the pigs.

After the months of feeding and sheltering the livestock, all that was left of the haystack was a heap of manure.

The manure was pitched into the spreader and spread over the field as
food for the grass.

And the grass grew tall in preparation for the cycle to begin again.